Cosmic Kidnappers

Cosmic Kidnappers

BY E.T. RANDALL

Illustrations by Jackie Rogers

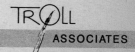
TROLL ASSOCIATES

Library of Congress Cataloging in Publication Data

Randall, E.T.
   Cosmic kidnappers.

   (Alien adventures)
   Summary: Drawn into a computer and out again into
an alien spaceship, the reader must figure out a way to get back home.
   1. Plot-your-own stories.   2. Children's stories,
American.   [1. Science fiction.   2. Plot-your-own
stories]   I. Rogers, Jacqueline, ill.   II. Title.   III. Series.
PZ7.R1564Co   1985   [Fic]   84-8579
ISBN 0-8167-0328-0 (lib. bdg.)
ISBN 0-8167-0329-9 (pbk.)

10   9   8   7   6   5   4   3   2   1

Before You Begin
Your Alien Adventure...

Remember—this is an out-of-this-world book. Start on page 1 and keep reading till you come to a choice. After that, the story is up to you. As you make decisions, your adventure will take you from page to page.

Think carefully before you decide! Some choices will lead you to exciting, heroic, and happy endings. But watch out! Other choices can quickly lead to disaster.

Now you're ready to begin. Best of luck in your **Alien Adventure!**

Cosmic Kidnappers

Social studies has never been your favorite subject. But you like it even less when you have to do your reports in the school's computer room. Julia Cramwell, the computer-room monitor, watches you like a hawk.

Today you are *really* bored. You wonder if Julia would notice if you slipped a game disk in your computer. She's stricter than most teachers are, and much better at catching you the few times you goof off. You hate having to come to the computer room when she's the monitor, especially since she's only a year older than you.

Without meaning to, your eyes meet hers. She says, "You have only fifteen more minutes to finish that satellite map report. Are you almost finished?"

You look at your totally blank screen. From behind you comes a triumphant giggle. You turn around and whisper to Norman Stillman, "You nerd. Stop crashing my computer!"

Turn to page 2.

Angrily you remove your disk with the map program on it, reinsert it, and start over.

Finally you find your place again. The screen says: TO ACCESS A LOCAL AREA MAP SHOWING THE LOCATION OF YOUR COMPUTER AND ANY OTHERS ON YOUR NETWORK, RAISE THE ANTENNA AT THE SIDE OF THE SCREEN AND PRESS *ENTER*.

You follow the instructions and a map appears. In the center of the screen is a square which must be the school. Inside the square, several lights flash on and off. You assume these lights are the computers in this room.

Beginning to feel drowsy, you remember you have to hand in a finished report in a matter of minutes. You sit up straight and wish maps weren't so deadly dull.

Behind the school on the map, you can make out the bleachers, and then the woods. This is strange. In the middle of the woods is another flashing light. What can that be? Who really cares?

Across the map you type onto the screen: I'M BORED. I WANT TO EXPERIMENT!

Suddenly the word EXPERIMENT flashes on and off and the screen reads:
EXPERIMENT—INTRUDER—INTERCEPTED
DO NOT CONTINUE

Go to page 3.

from page 2

Turning around, you whisper fiercely to Norman, "What are you up to now? I have to finish my report."

Norman is staring intently at his screen and doesn't reply. You lean over for a look. He's deep into a *Slithering Snakes* game and has already racked up a score of 11,285 points. So he is not playing a joke on you after all. Everyone else in the computer room looks equally busy.

Then you remember that flashing light in the woods. Could you have locked into a nearby computer? But what would one be doing behind the school? It doesn't make sense.

In your hand is a red magic marker that you've been doodling with on your note paper. Idly you tap it on the screen.

Instantly the marker begins to glow and the end that touched the screen slowly disintegrates. You snatch what's left of it away from the screen and put the stub in your pocket. While you're staring horrified at the screen, the bell rings. Everyone starts to leave for the next class.

If you try to make further contact via the computer turn to page 7.

If you go to the woods to see what's there, turn to page 43.

4

You refuse to promise not to escape. The rope alien winds itself around you and pulls you to the Containment Cabin where the rebels are confined.

But when the alien opens the door, rebels of every description pour out of the room.

Large spiderlike aliens scuttle down the hall. The rope alien releases you and chases after the spider creatures. But an alien like a flapping sheet flutters down the hall after it. The sheet wraps itself around the kicking, screaming rope alien and drags its prisoner back to the Containment Cabin.

You don't know what to do next.

"Hello, Earthling!" says a voice. You look up to see a mouth floating near the ceiling above you.

"I'm afraid the rest of me is invisible," the mouth says. "My name is Muklik. I've been in that cabin for a few hundred years and I've met some nice rebel Earthlings in that time. So come along with me. Don't be frightened."

Turn to page 54.

6

Slowly your finger moves down to the DELETE key.

You know that this is the key that erases what has been typed onto the computer screen. You hope it will either erase the program that controls the ship, or do something that will permit you to get away.

Firmly you press the DELETE key. Instantly, you, the craft, and all on board are erased from the face of the Earth without a trace.

THE END

from page 3

You type the message WHO ARE YOU? onto the screen and then press ENTER to send the message.

As soon as you touch the ENTER key, your finger turns a glowing red and disappears! You watch in frozen terror as your hand glows and disappears. Now your whole body feels prickly. For a moment, you have a feeling of drifting.

Then you are floating blindly in a dense fog. A deep voice says, "Earthling, you were warned. You have interrupted our experiments. We mean no harm to Earthlings, but our visit must remain a secret."

A sparkling blue jewel dangles in front of you. The voice says, "This jewel from the planet Marvella will be yours if you cooperate with us."

You feel dazed. It's hard to concentrate. What does the voice mean by cooperate? You have never before seen anything as beautiful as the jewel.

If you reach out for the jewel, turn to page 57.

If you hesitate, turn to page 28.

8

The uniformed man continues, "Tell Wallace to tell Nordeen to tell Statz to tell Conklin to tell Abner to tell Hanson to tell Fenstermeier to tell Jones that money MUST be found in the budget somehow!"

This man looks familiar, but it takes you a minute to realize who it is. He is someone you've seen on TV who's high up in the U.S. space program.

You look around again to see if anyone else is in the room. He certainly can't be talking to you. But you don't see anyone else.

Suddenly the man is gone! Now someone in a different uniform is shouting, and you can't understand a word he's saying!

Turn to page 108.

from page 111

A trip to the moon! Wow, will your friends be jealous!

After you are launched into space, you rush to a window and watch Earth getting smaller and smaller.

"We'll stop at the moon to let you off. You can catch the next ship back," Borius says.

"What ship?" you ask.

"Surely Earth has regularly scheduled transportation to the moon? It's so close to Earth," Borius says.

You sit down in a state of shock.

"I wish I had known," Borius says. "If you have no way of getting home, you'd better stay with us. I don't know our schedule exactly, but we should return to Earth by 3,000 A.D. on your calendar at the latest. At least you can send a message home if you like."

Borius takes you to a bank of computers in the communications room. "We have entered all Earth's electronic communications services. In case we ever decide to take over your planet, it will save us a great deal of time," he says matter-of-factly.

He enters some numbers on the keyboard, and the screen fills with directions. After entering a few more numbers in response, he tells you to write whatever you want and it will appear on your computer screen at your home.

Turn to page 99.

10

from page 78

You stay and learn more about the lizards.

Unfortunately, the spaceship never comes back for you.

The giant lizards soon lose their fear of you, and a lizard family takes you in as their pet person. In the beginning, they tie a vine to you and take you for long walks. You discover that the planet has a varied landscape, including grassy areas and forests. But the lizards prefer the mud.

Finally they let you roam freely. With the help of your translator box, you learn Lizardese. Sometimes a lizard lets you ride on its back as it leaps SLAP SLAP SLAP through the mud. But try as hard as they will to teach you, you never are able to leap quickly through the mud on your own.

Twenty years later, a spaceship from Earth lands and the crew is astounded to find you. Deciding to return to Earth, you bid a reluctant farewell to your slimy friends.

Reunited with your friends and family at home, you write a phenomenal best seller, *My Life in Lizard Land*.

THE END

You don't want to be Julia's assistant and you tell her so. You don't tell her you will try to escape at any opportunity.

"Suit yourself," she says.

Suddenly aliens grab you from behind and strap you to the pole again.

Minutes later the ship takes off. When you are well out in space, Julia releases the three of you. She tells you to stay in this room until she finds spacesuits for you, so you can breathe in the other areas. Then she leaves through the tunnel. While Norman is pounding frantically on the walls, you look carefully around the empty room. Mrs. Hardline joins you.

In the walls are indentations that could be buttons. Should you press one? Mrs. Hardline shrugs her shoulders and says, "Our situation couldn't be much worse, could it?"

You don't know. Holding your breath, you put your finger into the hole in one wall.

Turn to page 104.

Before you and Strallie jump ship, you leave a sealed note for your parents with a friendly steward. The note says you have to disappear for a while because you have a responsibility to help someone.

You are glad the ship is docking at night. As the ship nears the lights on the pier, you and Strallie stand submissively on deck under the watchful eye of the first mate. Suddenly you both run for the railing and leap over the side of the ship.

There is a great deal of yelling and confusion on board. But with your long arms and Strallie's big feet, you manage to make it to shore and disappear in the darkness.

After a long journey, you see Strallie happily settled with her new friends in the Australian outback. An aborigine leads you back to port where your parents are waiting. They are happy to know you are safe.

THE END

14

You decide to keep the jewel. You might as well go through with what you agreed to do. What harm can there be in a few people talking to the visitors from space?

When you come in the back door of the school, the first person you see is Julia Cramwell. You don't want to bring this know-it-all to the spaceship.

She bars your way. "So you were skipping class?" she says. "Come with me to the principal's office."

She's taller than you and pretty strong. Though you want to get away, you know it would only get you into worse trouble. You follow Julia right into the office of Mrs. Hardline, the principal. Her real name is Mrs. Harding, but she's always getting up in assembly on Wednesdays and talking about what will happen to students after they graduate if they don't knuckle down in school. Every speech ends with her favorite saying, "Suffer now or suffer later."

Stammering, you try to come up with an excuse. Then you remember you have a solution in your hand.

Holding out the jewel, you say, "Come!"

As you walk out of the room, Mrs. Hardline and Julia follow you without question.

Turn to page 31.

from page 106

Somehow you must keep the aliens from returning to their home planet and reporting that Earth is ripe for invasion. But what can you do to stop the ship from taking off?

The rope alien says, "If you will promise not to try to escape from the ship, you may go to the Apprentice Learning Lab. Otherwise you will be confined to the Containment Cabin with the other rebels who think of nothing but getting away. These creatures cause no end of commotion. What do you say? If you give me your word without meaning it, I will know and you will be tossed out into space."

Your mind is filled with impossible plans for preventing the ship from leaving. But before you have a chance to reply, you suddenly feel the ship take off. So much for your plans.

The alien is still waiting for an answer. If there is any chance to escape, you want to take it. On the other hand, you could stop the aliens from reaching home if you could get at the ship's controls and sabotage them. But you certainly can't do that while confined to one room.

If you promise not to try to escape, turn to page 101.

If you refuse to promise, turn to page 4.

16

Before you can plan your escape, a door in one wall slides open. Some shiny-looking creatures enter the room. Everything about these creatures looks and smells like they are covered with oil—their skin, their hair, their long flowing clothes.

"Takeoff!" Mrs. Hardline exclaims. "In that case, these young people and I will be leaving. You have no right to keep us."

There is no reply from the Voice. But one of the aliens goes to the door to the outside and begins to shut it.

You are not going to stand around arguing. Even though the alien is bigger than you are, your only chance is to make a break for it.

Mrs. Hardline is still objecting vehemently. You lower your head and run at the alien like a battering ram.

Turn to page 80.

18

You know that the RESET key clears the computer and allows you to start over from scratch when things go wrong.

Hoping that this will make it possible for you to program the computer to do what you want, you press down on the RESET key.

The aliens immediately disappear from sight. Even your memory of them is completely wiped out. All recollection of this entire incident is gone.

Turn to page 1.

from page 87

Taking a deep breath, you stare at the red and yellow disks. You aren't aware of being hypnotized.

The next thing you know, you are staring at the satellite map on your computer at school. Feeling incredibly relaxed, you let out a great yawn. Your face turns red as you realize you yawned out loud. Everyone is staring at you.

Suddenly, out of the blue, the thought comes to you that some day you'd like to travel to outer space. You'd better pay more attention to this map stuff.

THE END

20

As you scramble to your feet, the sounds get louder.

What you see almost makes you laugh. The creature has the body of a kangaroo and the head of a koala.

You stare at each other for a moment. Finally it says, "My name is Strallie. You look harmless. Are you?"

"Yes, I am," you say. "Are you from that thing?" you ask, pointing to the craft.

"Yes," says Strallie. "They kidnapped me from a planet very far away from here. And they say I can never return. I've been to your planet several times before. That's how I learned your language. But this is the first time I've had a chance to escape. I've heard that some of my ancestors escaped here long, long ago. But I don't know what happened to them."

"I think I know where they are," you say.

Strallie says, "Do you think if I was on my own I would be treated well here? Or could I come and stay with you?"

You know that everyone would want to get a look at the first alien to settle on Earth. This gentle creature could be hurt even by well-meaning people. But perhaps you could hide her and keep her safe.

If you tell Strallie you don't know if she would like it here, turn to page 112.

If you say that you will hide her, turn to page 26.

from page 111

You'd like to go to the moon but not on an alien ship. "I want to leave," you insist.

As you stand by the door, Borius presses a button above it that you didn't even notice.

"Permission to let visitor out," Borius says.

You can't see an intercom, but a voice fills the room: EARTHLING, YOU WILL BE ALLOWED TO LEAVE. BUT FIRST YOU MUST UNDERSTAND THAT EARTH IS A PRIMITIVE PLANET. ITS INHABITANTS ARE STILL LIVING IN THE AGE OF AGGRESSION. THOSE OF US WHO ARE COOPERATING ON THIS MISSION ARE FROM GALAXIES WHICH SURVIVED THIS STAGE EONS AGO.

"I'm not aggressive," you say. But the voice keeps speaking.

EARTHLINGS HAVE NOT EVOLVED HIGHLY ENOUGH TO BE ALLOWED TO COLONIZE IN SPACE YET. WE CANNOT ALLOW YOU TO CAUSE WIDESPREAD RUINATION. YOU MUST BE STOPPED.

"Now look, whoever you are! You don't have the right to harm us," you shout aggressively.

Turn to page 72.

from page 99

Zax is delighted to have you for an apprentice. He proudly shows you all his machines.

"I designed and built these all by myself," he says. "This machine uses energy from the sun to pass an electric current through rocks to release oxygen. The spaceship you came on stopped by to get oxygen to mix with its fuel."

Zax moves a distance away to another huge machine. "This is the one I want you to work on. Keep an eye on this bucket and let me know when it's full," he tells you.

Rocks and rubble on a conveyer belt fall into a huge bucket at the end of an enormous metal arm.

"What's it for?" you ask.

Zax's eyes sparkle through his long hair as he explains. "I have this all worked out mathematically. The long arm will spin around and fling the rocks into space. In reaction, the little asteroid we're on will move in the opposite direction. We'll keep flinging rocks out until our asteroid hits a comet which is due to pass near the moon. Our crash will make the comet collide with the moon."

"We're going to crash?" you ask in alarm.

Turn to page 100.

You press down on the PAUSE key, hoping it will keep the aliens frozen and give you time to think about what to do next.

As soon as you lift your finger, you are no longer on the ship. All you can see are millions of tiny, dazzling lights. You are floating weightlessly. It is a pleasant feeling, but you feel incredibly lonely.

You almost cry for joy when you see in the distance a dim shape that becomes clearer as it approaches you.

"Hello, newcomer," calls out a round, purple alien. "Obviously you're an Earthling. I was just talking to some Earthlings who say they came here from a place called the Bermuda Triangle."

"Oh!" you say. "Does that mean we're dead?"

"No, no," says the alien. "We are somewhere outside of time, between life and death. Now and then one of us disappears to go back to time. Or beyond it— I really don't know which. Everyone is friendly here, so come along and meet the others. You won't feel so lonely when you get to know some of us."

Hearing cheerful voices in the distance, you follow your new friend.

THE END

26

You take Strallie home and hide her in the safest place you can think of—the garage. It's so full of junk that your parents have to park their cars in front of the house. You're the only one who goes near the garage, to put your bike away or to get out the lawn mower.

You teach Strallie to play checkers and chess, and spend as much time as you can with her. But one day she says, "Thank you for protecting me. But I don't want to hide here or play games anymore. I either want to do something useful or to go to the place where my ancestors settled."

Seeing the tears in her eyes, you realize Strallie is terribly unhappy.

If you tell her you will take her where her ancestors settled, turn to page 29.

If you say you will find something for her to do, turn to page 84.

from page 112

You can't wait to see the inside of the spaceship.

Strallie jumps up the ladder to the door and opens it. After looking inside, she beckons for you to follow.

Eagerly you climb the ladder and step inside the ship, wondering what you'll see.

What awaits you is the last thing you expect. You are in a small room full of two-faced creatures. All of them have a little hair standing straight up from the top of their heads. Since their feet are round and they can walk in either direction, it's impossible to tell which is their front and which is their back.

Fortunately only Strallie is between you and the door. You make a run for it, counting on her to help you.

Instead, she grabs your collar and pushes you at the aliens!

"Strallie, help me!" you yell. To your shock, she removes her costume and turns out to be one of them!

"I got one," she says to the others. "I told you it would work."

Turn to page 61.

from page 7

You start to reach out for the jewel, then hesitate.

YOU HAD YOUR CHANCE, EARTHLING, says the Voice as the jewel disappears. SO YOU CAN'T MAKE UP YOUR MIND? RIGHT NOW I CANNOT MAKE UP MY MIND ABOUT WHAT TO DO WITH *YOU*. I HAVE MORE IMPORTANT THINGS TO THINK ABOUT.

It is quiet for so long that you wonder if you will ever experience anything again but silence and fog. At last the haze clears, and you discover that you are floating in a small room. Through a window, you see trees and your school in the distance. Beneath the window you see a bank of computers inside the room.

By a closed door stand two aliens in spacesuits. They have their backs to you and are talking in a strange language. One has six heads and the other five.

Maybe you can get out of the window somehow while they aren't looking. But when you try to swim through the air to it, all you do is turn somersaults!

By touching one wall with your fingers, you inch along toward the window and grasp the frame to pull yourself closer. Oh, no! This window wasn't made to open. Using your feet, you pull yourself down onto a computer, accidentally pressing a key.

Turn to page 110.

from page 26

That night, leaving a note for your parents, you and Strallie go down to the docks. You wear your Halloween monster outfit on top of your regular clothes. When people stop to stare at the pair of you, you tell them you're on your way to a costume party. Finally you find a ship ready to set off for Australia.

You always dreamed about stowing away on a ship, and you know just what to do. As passengers and the people seeing them off board the ship, the two of you stroll up the gangplank with them. Once on board, you head for the lifeboats. When no one is looking, you and Strallie climb into one.

"See how easy it is?" you tell Strallie.

The whistle blows, the guests get off, and the ship leaves the dock. You and Strallie enjoy peeking out of the covered lifeboat to watch the reflection of the moon on the water. Soon you both fall asleep.

In the morning you discover a hitch in your plan. You are terribly hungry.

Telling Strallie to stay put, you take off your monster costume and search the ship for food. There's plenty of food around. But in your crumpled clothes, you look out of place. A steward asks, "With which family are you traveling?"

Turn to page 75.

30

from page 108

You decide to look around the ship a little more. If someone catches you, you always have your school paper excuse. The only problem is you can't find any other door besides the one you came in. Then you spot what could be a door near the floor. When you put your finger in a small indentation, you find the door slides open. You can just barely crawl through to another room.

When you can stand up, you find the room is filled with rows of cages. In one cage is a bear cub, in another a tiny evergreen tree in a pot. There is even a tiny cage with a butterfly in it. Further back the cages hold creatures completely unfamiliar to you.

Suddenly you hear something fluttering behind you. You turn to see a being made of tiny red and yellow disks. The disks are all shaking and trembling at once.

"Oh, good, good, good," the thing says. "A volunteer! You would not believe how seldom this happens. I believe the last time was on the planet Xorxus 354 years ago. Or was it 543? No, I think it was 435 years. I can check my records. Anyway, it is so much nicer than having to use force. I'll let you pick out your own cage."

Turn to page 87.

from page 14

You and Julia and Mrs. Hardline walk down the hall like follow-the-leader.

Students are milling around between classes, but they hurry away when they see Mrs. Hardline. All except Norman Stillman, who is staring at the jewel and doesn't notice her.

You are definitely not going to tell Norman to come. But as you approach him, he automatically sticks out his leg to trip you.

Before you can stop yourself, you say, *"Come* off it, Stillman." He falls into step behind Mrs. Hardline. The four of you march out of school and through the woods to the spaceship.

As soon as you step inside the ship, the jewel disappears from your hand. The others all start talking at once. Mrs. Hardline holds up her hand for silence and says to you, "What are we doing here? I thought you had some problem for me to take care of."

You look around, bewildered. You are in a small empty room. A fly buzzes annoyingly around your head.

A voice that makes the walls vibrate says, "EARTHLINGS, YOU ARE HERE TO ANSWER QUESTIONS, NOT TO ASK THEM."

If you decide to be silent, turn to page 107.

If you insist on asking how long you will be here, turn to page 40.

32

You hesitate, then press down on the red key—complete planetary change.

Immediately you find yourself studying at the Future Pickle-Packers Training Institute. The course is stimulating, but not difficult. There are no tests or homework.

At 3:12 p.m. on Mondays, Wednesdays, and Fridays, you ride your bike. On the other days you swim. After 72 days of swimming, you will study snorkeling for four weeks, after which you will move on to diving.

At 5:02 p.m. you sit down to a wholesome, balanced dinner. After supper, you play the oboe, then relax with your new hobby of making pictures out of buttons you've collected. You will pursue this hobby for the next three years, five months, and seventeen days.

Every moment of your new life is programmed, and you are never unhappy, surprised, or excited. You don't even know how bored you are.

THE END

34

from page 43

You jump up to catch the bottom rung of the ladder and pull yourself up. The door at the top is closed, and there is no way to look inside the ship. You are about to knock on the door, but just in time you realize you'd better have a good reason for being here.

But what could your reason be? The school paper—that's it! You can say you're doing a story on this strange craft. And that's no lie. The school editor would love to get a scoop on this, beating out the town daily.

But there's no answer to your knock. You start to climb down the ladder. Then you pause. You'll be kicking yourself the rest of your life if you don't at least see if the door is unlocked and take a peek inside.

You try to turn the latch, but it doesn't budge. In frustration, you give it a good hard push. The door opens.

You enter a tiny room. In a corner you see a man in uniform who is saying, "We must set up a permanent space colony before THEY do!" He seems to be talking to a blank wall.

Wow! What did you walk into?

If you decide to get out before anyone catches you there, turn to page 58.

If you decide to ask if you can interview him for your school paper, turn to page 8.

You set the controls that you believe will bring the ship close enough to get a good look at the planet.

Unfortunately your programming brings the ship so close that it gets a gravity boost from the planet, flinging the ship way off course and back toward Earth.

When the ship is sailing smoothly again, the aliens put you on trial. The only excuse you can offer is that you were curious about the colorful planet. You apologize for putting the ship in danger.

The aliens decide you are too reckless to remain on board. But as long as they're in the neighborhood, they take you home.

You've been gone a few years, but in space you didn't age much. You are now younger than your kid brother. After the excitement of your return dies down, he gets very bossy.

But after space-program experts seek you out for advice about alien psychology, you hear your brother bragging about you to his friends.

THE END

"YOU WILL LONG REGRET YOUR MISTAKE, EARTH-
LING!" roars the Voice. "FORTUNATELY ONE OF YOUR
COMPANIONS WARNED ME AND I FOUND AN ALTERNATE
MODE OF TRANSPORT."

You glare at Norman who says, "I didn't do it!"

Then you both freeze as the biggest bumblebee
you're ever seen buzzes around your heads.

"I told," Julia says. "Your plan was clumsy. To
avoid even worse trouble, I feel the logical thing to do
is to cooperate with our captors."

The trip to the moon doesn't take long. Julia is put
in charge of your group. Alongside aliens of every description, the three of you help dig a foundation for a
moon town.

When Julia catches Norman trying to look busy
without actually doing any work, she makes you work
all the harder. Finally you say, "It isn't fair that you're
in charge and don't have to work."

She says, "O.K., I'll put you in charge of Norman.
If you can get him to do his share of the work and your
own share too, fine. But if he doesn't work, you have to
do his share and yours too."

Try as you might, you can't persuade Norman to
do any work at all.

*If you ask Mrs. Hardline to help you with Norman,
turn to page 91.*

If you keep trying to persuade Norman, turn to page 98.

from page 46

At first you are well-treated on Vallius, but finally your novelty value wears thin. You are ignored and bored.

When you hear of an expedition setting out that will include Earth in its itinerary, you beg Hexter to take you along. He agrees.

Back on Earth, you are quickly recognized as an authority on space travel. You are asked to lecture at universities all over the world.

It feels good not to be a "primitive representative" anymore!

THE END

from page 108

As you head for the door, you try to figure out the best way to contact someone in the U.S. space program. Maybe you should go to the FBI. Or would the CIA handle something like this?

But before you can reach the door, you hear a noise above you. You look up to see an opening in the ceiling. A long-haired creature descends smoothly to the floor on a platform that has no sides or cables.

She is staring at you with her one huge eye in the middle of her square face. As you stare back, her eye seems to grow larger and larger and paler and paler until you seem to be enclosed in a hazy grayness.

Suddenly you are sitting in front of a computer at school, feeling a little dizzy. In the back of your mind, some worry is nagging at you. But you can't remember what it is you're trying to remember. Somehow you feel you've lost a little time somewhere. But how can that be? All you've been doing is sitting in front of this computer. Haven't you?

THE END

40

"I feel responsible for these people because I brought them," you say. "How long do you expect us to stay here answering questions?" You sound a lot bolder than you feel. The fly starts buzzing around your head again and you swat at it.

"BEWARE! YOU HAVE THE AUDACITY TO TRY TO KILL ME, YOU MERE EARTHLING?" thunders the Voice in tones so tremendous that you are almost knocked off your feet.

"Sorry!" you apologize. "All I did was swat at a fly!" Then a thought hits you. "You're not—I mean, that fly isn't—isn't *you*, is it?"

"OF COURSE NOT," roars the Voice. "THAT IS A RIDICULOUS NOTION, EVEN FROM AN EARTHLING."

"Oh. I'm sorry," you say. The last thing you want to do is offend this thing.

The Voice goes on, "THE FLY IS MERELY ONE OF MY MODES OF TRANSPORTATION. NOW THAT WE HAVE YOU TO REPLACE SOME WORKERS WHO COLLAPSED FROM EXHAUSTION AT OUR MOON BASE, I MUST PREPARE THE SHIP FOR TAKEOFF!"

Thoroughly terrified, you know you must get out of here in a hurry.

If you try to escape on your own, turn to page 16.

If you take the added risk of trying to help the others escape, turn to page 62.

"The most important thing to remember is not to teleport yourself outside the ship," S-Mog says. "We probably wouldn't be able to find you."

In a small, soundless chamber, you learn to concentrate as you never have before. Your first success comes when you manage to move yourself just outside the room. You try to run to tell S-Mog. But your foot is still inside the chamber. S-Mog has to chop a hole around it to free you.

After that you are able to move yourself—through concentration—to other parts of the ship. You secretly begin to look for the steering controls so you can sabotage them. S-Mog tells you the other aliens are complaining. You will have your brain cleared of all past memory patterns, including what you've learned about Teleportation, if you don't behave.

Moving yourself in and out of the chamber soon gets boring. One day, homesickness overwhelms you.

Suddenly you find you are in your room at home, having teleported yourself there. Immediately you write a long letter to the government, telling them about the alien danger to Earth.

You don't receive an official reply. But you do get a phone call from a "Mr. Smith" who thanks you for your help. He says the aliens probably changed their plans after you returned to Earth in time to give a warning.

THE END

42

"I guess we're sort of typical," you say, hoping that's the right answer.

"Good!" booms the voice, sounding pleased. You breathe a sigh of relief.

The next thing you know, several aliens in spacesuits come in and start strapping each of you to a pole in a different corner of the room. At least you assume they are aliens. You can't see what they look like. All four of you start yelling at the aliens to stop tying you up.

The Voice rumbles, "You must come to our planet. There you will be put in our museum of typical life examples from other galaxies. Any of you who do not go quietly will be put on display as stuffed specimens."

Immediately you all decide to be silent.

"That is better. We must go now to prepare for takeoff," the Voice says.

As soon as you see the aliens leave through a hatch in one wall, you struggle to get out of the straps. You notice that Julia has already freed herself.

"Relax," she tells you. "I'll take care of this."

You know Julia is very smart. You also know it would be extremely dangerous to get caught trying to escape. You try to decide what to do in this desperate situation.

If you let Julia handle it, turn to page 95.

If you try your own way, turn to page 50.

from page 3

In ten seconds you are out the computer-room door, down the hall, and outside the back door of the school building.

You race through the small lawn and around the bleachers, hoping no one sees you leaving.

When you reach the woods just behind the bleachers, you slow down, partly because you are out of breath, but also because something tells you that you ought to be cautious.

Slowly and quietly you go from tree to tree. Even though you are expecting something unusual, the sight in the clearing takes your breath away.

There is a three-legged round object that can only be a spaceship. How else could it get there? It doesn't have helicopter blades.

A ladder reaches almost to the ground, and no one seems to be around.

If you climb the ladder, turn to page 34.

If you stay hidden and keep watching, turn to page 93.

44

from page 113

When the rope creature finally slithers back through the hole in the wall, you moan and groan and say, "I think I have the highly contagious, red-dotted plague!"

The rope alien hastily retreats out of the room. The next thing you know, you feel the spaceship descend and then softly land.

A trap door opens in the floor. The rope alien guides you to the cargo bay and gives you a shove out the door.

You are overjoyed, until you see you are on an incredibly high mountain peak with no civilization in sight. Looking down one side, you wonder if you can climb down the steep slope.

From the other side of the peak, you hear human voices! You turn to see two mountain climbers.

"How did you get here?" one man asks, as if in a state of shock. "We thought we were the first ones to make it."

They refuse to believe your story. But they do help you climb down the mountain.

When you get home at last, no one will believe you went up in a spaceship and climbed down a mountain—all in one day.

THE END

You allow the ship to continue on course. Eventually you reach the home planet, Vallius, of the expedition's leader, Hexter.

Vallius is a sparsely inhabited planet with no buildings over one story high. Everyone has his or her own little, round house, even the children. Instead of individual televisions, there are huge sky screens on which everyone watches the same programs.

You appear frequently on the sky-screen interview shows. While at first this is exciting, after a while you are annoyed at being constantly introduced as a representative of life on a primitive planet.

Turn to page 37.

from page 75

You explain to Strallie how you can help her escape if you stay on board. When she is ready to jump ship, you run around and scream to distract everyone's attention. It works—on everyone but the captain, who is watching Strallie and thinking about all the money he is going to get from the zoo. Just before she is ready to jump for freedom, the captain grabs her.

The ship docks and your parents come on board just in time to hear the captain say to Strallie, "Time for you to go to the zoo, mate."

You and Strallie look at each other with tears in your eyes. You turn away and see your mother looking at you and Strallie and the captain. She seems to be putting two and two together.

Finally she says sharply, "The two of you were very wrong to run off like that. So you just march off this ship and we'll take the next plane home." Taking your hand and Strallie's paw, she starts leading you both away.

Picking up on this, your father quickly tells the captain, "Thanks for taking care of our kids. Just send us a bill for their fare."

"Your kids?" cries the captain. "Both of them?"

But by then you and Strallie and your parents are halfway down the gangplank, on your way home.

THE END

48

from page 61

"O.K.," you say. "I'll find someone else to take my place." But you don't really mean it. All you want to do is get out of the spaceship. Suddenly school seems like a wonderful place to be—a safe haven.

Standing between you and the door, Strallie says sharply, "Look me in the eye!"

You try to look at Strallie, but every time you almost make contact, your eyes veer away. You can't control them! Is this some kind of alien test?

Next thing you know, you are being strapped to a pole. By the time they unstrap you and you are able to get to a window, you have an excellent view of the far side of the moon!

THE END

from page 101

The gray-haired alien introduces itself as S-Mog and explains, "In the Transport Division, you have a choice of Teleportation or Matter Transmission. In other words, you can choose between moving yourself or moving objects."

S-Mog turns a knob. On the wall appears a film, narrated in English.

As you watch, you find the movie is like the educational films at school. The film is called, "Why Teleportation and Matter Transmission?" During the next two hours, you get a detailed history of Teleportation and Matter Transmission, dwelling especially on the early eons of their development.

When the film is over, S-Mog asks which skill you'd like to study further. Since you slept through most of the film, you don't dare ask any questions.

If you choose Teleportation, turn to page 41.

If you choose Matter Transmission, turn to page 86.

You decide to do it your way. Julia disappears through the hatch in the wall without waiting to free the rest of you.

With agonizing slowness you inch one arm up and out of the strap and gradually free yourself. You consider releasing Norman and Mrs. Hardline, but don't want to lose any more time. Norman might be more hindrance than help anyway.

You open the hatch and climb into a tunnel. The passage is so low, you can only crawl slowly through it. Finally you reach another hatch. Cautiously, you open it a sliver and peek through.

A group of aliens wearing orange uniforms are sitting in a circle on the floor, looking at what must be navigational charts. Without their spacesuits, they look somewhat like Earth people, except for their purple hair.

You are all the more surprised when one of them makes an angry comment in some alien language, and then retracts its head inside its body like a turtle. Another alien, the only one with black hair instead of purple, reaches out to point to a chart and then pulls its arm inside its body. When that alien turns to speak to the one next to it, its face comes into view, and you gasp.

It's Julia in an orange uniform!

Turn to page 116.

52

from page 113

You try to think of some way to stop the aliens. But before you can come up with a plan, the strange rope creature comes back.

It takes one look at your red-dotted skin and says, "I am getting so confused! I thought I left an Earthling in here but you're obviously an escapee. Come now, you must go back to your cell."

The rope creature ties one end of itself around you and pulls you right through the little hole in the wall. You are surprised that it doesn't hurt—in fact, it tickles. Then the creature leads you down a maze of extremely narrow corridors, opens a door, and nudges you into a room. The door closes behind you.

You are in a room full of glowing green creatures with arms down to the floor, all of them covered with red dots. The aliens are all alike except that those on one side of the room are about seven feet tall, and those gathered on the other side are shorter than you.

They all stare at you. One of the tall ones says, "It's not one of *us*."

Another tall one looks at the short creatures on the other side of the room and says, "But it's not one of *them*. It might be interesting. Let's let it talk to us and see!"

Some of the short creatures call out to you, "We'd love to have you join us. Please do!"

If you go over to the tall creatures, turn to page 66.

If you join the short creatures, turn to page 92.

You are gently but firmly shoved out a door, along with a box of food and a tent.

When you drop from the bottom rung of the ladder, you find yourself ankle-deep in mud. You hurry to get away from the ship so you won't be burned when it takes off.

Carrying your supplies, you head for one of the huge boulders—the only things to be seen in the dreary, gray landscape. PLOCK, you raise one foot out of the muck. PLOCK, PLOCK, PLOCK. Walking is such an effort that you don't even turn when the ship takes off. A feeling of loneliness overwhelms you.

You forget about it in an instant when you round the boulder and meet a huge, slimy lizard with burning, red eyes.

Now what? Should you try to scare the lizard? Or should you freeze and hope it realizes you're harmless?

If you look the lizard in the eye, and yell and wave your arms, turn to page 64.

If you freeze and look away, turn to page 78.

54

from page 4

As you start to follow Muklik down the hall, you trip over a rock.

"Ouch! Watch where you're going!" the rock says.

"Oops, sorry," you say, jumping over it. The rock rolls along behind you.

It's hard to follow a mouth. But you stay as close to Muklik as you can. You and Muklik help the other rebels take over the ship.

Since Earth is the closest planet, the rebels take you home first. On the way, you ask Muklik about her planet.

"I was very young when I was captured," Muklik says. "I don't think anyone I know will still be alive on my planet. I hardly remember it. But I love to hear about Earth."

By the time you land in a field near your house, you and Muklik are good friends.

You're glad to be home, but it's hard to say good-by to your new friend. With tears in your eyes, you wave as the spaceship takes off.

Then you run home, not noticing a giggling sound from a mouth floating high above you.

THE END

from page 81

Between going to school by day and having Robert secretly coach you at night, you whiz through school. You are graduated from Engineering College at the age of fifteen.

You get a job designing robots for factories and homes. Soon you head the company. Representatives from governments all over the world come to see your robot designs. Everyone smiles at your cute little brother who is always at your side, even though—as everyone says—he couldn't possibly understand all those blueprints.

THE END

56

The aliens on the ship welcome you back on board. Now you are allowed to go anywhere you please on the ship. Your favorite spot is at the window in the Computer Control Room where you can see what's ahead.

Since you take such an interest, the aliens let you watch them at the computer controls. You become friends with Galastrian, a short alien with a body as lean as a broomstick. She has green, fuzzy skin and enormous feet on her three legs.

Galastrian, as the Steering-Computer Standby, has the job of making sure the computer that sets the directional course for the spaceship is in working order. In the unlikely event that the computer and its malfunction alarm stop working at the same time, she is to seek help before the spaceship goes off course.

One day, when Galastrian has to attend a lecture, her replacement doesn't arrive on time. She asks you to keep an eye on the computer.

After watching the computer for a while, you glance out the window and see what looks like a planet with many-colored rings around it. You know how to work the computer controls by now, and you wish you could get a closer look at it.

If you make the computer steer the spaceship closer for a better look, turn to page 35.

If you don't want to mess around with the computer, turn to page 46.

Before you can grasp the jewel, the voice says, "By accepting the jewel, you agree to recruit other Earthlings and bring them here."

"What if nobody wants to come?" you ask.

The voice says, "When you carry the jewel, whomever you say the word COME to will be unable to resist following you here."

You are still fighting to think clearly, though your brain feels like cotton. "Then what will happen to us?" you mumble, getting the words out with difficulty.

The voice says, "We just want to talk to several Earthlings. We want to learn about your culture and your attitudes toward those from other galaxies."

If you accept the space jewel, turn to page 102.

If you refuse to accept the jewel until you can see who is speaking, turn to page 109.

58

You dash to the door to get out before you are seen. But the door won't open.

Hearing a noise behind you, you whirl around. No one is there—only some odd-looking furniture and a few pictures on the walls.

One of the pictures catches your eye. It is a painting of a blue tree with orange leaves. Did something move in the leaves? Before your eyes, the tree grows larger and floats out of the frame. It floats down to the floor and goes over to a box near the man in uniform. Using a branch, it depresses a button on the box. Instantly, the man in uniform disappears. The tree clumps toward you on short, gnarled roots.

"That man was just a picture!" you say to the tree. "It sure looked real! But...but what are you? You must be a picture, too!"

"Am I?" asks the tree, touching the top of your head with a branch that feels quite solid.

Turn to page 111.

60

from page 81

You look forward to going to school now. With Robert doing all your homework, it will be a breeze.

Your parents know that Robert is a robot, but they have trouble remembering it. Soon they treat him as the three-year-old he appears to be. When they aren't around, Robert mows the lawn for you, takes out the garbage, and does all the rest of your chores.

Now that Robert is doing your homework, you hand in perfect assignments every time. Your teachers are delighted.

But the bubble bursts when you have a week of tests and you do miserably. After that, you have to do extra work every night until you catch up. And the lady next door complains about your little brother having to mow the lawn.

But it's still fun having Robert around. He loves to play video games with you.

THE END

Strallie tells you, "There is no way to escape, so you may as well relax. You will be well-treated and your work won't be difficult."

"You don't have any right to kidnap me," you say angrily. "What do you need me for anyway? There are plenty of you."

"We need your fingers," Strallie says. Then you notice that their hands have only a thumb and one wide, round finger.

"When our ship broke, we borrowed this craft from another galaxy. The repair work can best be done by fingers like yours," she continues. "Our hands are too clumsy for making some of the finer adjustments. Cheer up. It won't be so bad. You'll find us quite pleasant and civilized."

"Strallie, I liked you. I trusted you!" you say. "There must be some way I can get out of going into space."

"I don't like doing it this way. But we must have a repair technician with us," Strallie says.

She confers with the others in a strange tongue. Then she tells you, "There is only one way. You can stay on Earth if you find us another Earthling to take your place."

"I'll do it! I promise!" you say.

If you really mean to find someone, turn to page 96.

If you plan to forget your promise as soon as you get away, turn to page 48.

62

from page 40

You want to help everyone escape the ship. But before you can make a move, a trap door in the floor opens. Into the room climb strange creatures that look like small pyramids. They only come up to your shoulders and they seem to roll about rather than walk. You see the fly going from one to another.

The four of you huddle in a corner. Searching your pockets for inspiration, you try to think of an escape plan. A rubber band offers a brief hope but even Norman, who's had the most shooting practice in school, can't aim well enough to hit that fly.

The little box of raisins left over from your lunch gives you an idea. "I'm going to open this box and put it on the floor," you say. "If that's a regular fly, it can't resist raisins. As soon as it goes inside, I'll close the box with my foot and that thing that's riding the fly will be stuck inside. It may cause enough confusion for us to get out the door. You see if you can distract those pyramid things."

Julia and Norman say together, "It won't work!"

"Anything is worth a try," Mrs. Hardline says.

The others move away as you put the box down. Eventually the fly buzzes around it for a moment and goes inside. In your eagerness to close the box, you stomp on it with your foot and quickly step back terrified. What happened to the fly and its rider? What will happen to you?

Turn to page 36.

from page 84

"Hey, wait!" says Chuck. "I've been racking my brain trying to come up with the perfect gimmick. That costume is better than anything I could have dreamed up."

"Huh?" you say.

"I'm opening up a chain of Chuck's Chickenburgers, and I wanted some symbol to attract new customers. You know, like a trademark." Chuck's excitement builds. "I'll call you Kangawalla the Koalaroo," he says to Strallie. "Together, we'll make Roo Burgers the people's choice from coast to coast!" Strallie gets excited, too.

She starts her new career by standing on the street and greeting passers-by. She is so popular that Chuck asks her to appear at the opening of every new Chickenburger restaurant. The rest is history. Children come from everywhere to meet Strallie and enjoy Roo Burgers. In fact, her first national tour earns her enough money to buy the house next door to yours!

Strallie becomes a household name because of her Chuck's Chickenburger TV commercials. Thinking she wears a costume, people smile whenever they see her on the street. Only you know the truth—and you never give away Strallie's secret.

THE END

from page 53

Making horrible, fierce expressions, you scream, "I'm not afraid of you!" You hope the creature won't notice how much you're shaking.

The lizard almost bursts your eardrums with an enormous roar.

In your pocket, the translator box squawks: WORD NOT IN MY VOCABULARY, BUT TONE WOULD SEEM TO EXPRESS ANGER.

You try to turn and run but you can barely move in the mud. The beast swallows you in one gulp, and makes a happy sound.

Deep inside its stomach, the translator box squawks: MMM-DELICIOUS!

THE END

"Uh, no, we're not very typical. Most people—I mean Earthlings—are much more typical than we are. Probably," you say, ready to take it all back if the Voice seems angry.

Instead, the Voice sounds disappointed. "I AM AFRAID THAT MEANS YOU CAN'T COME WITH US. WE ARE ONLY COLLECTING TYPICAL PLANETARIAN LIFE SAMPLES ON THIS TRIP. MAYBE NEXT TIME."

You're afraid to rush to the door, but Norman is shoving you from behind. You almost fall down the ladder. As soon as you are in the woods out of sight of the spaceship, you all start to run. Then you hear the ship take off with a gigantic roar.

In the days that follow, the four of you exchange glances, but you don't dare speak of what happened. Who would believe you?

You breathe a sigh of relief whenever you remember that you could be speeding through the universe, perhaps never to return home.

One good thing did come out of this experience: Julia Cramwell and Norman Stillman are now afraid to have anything to do with you. They will never give you a hard time again.

THE END

66

from page 52

You introduce yourself to the tall creatures. Instead of replying, they stare at you.

The silent stares make you nervous. Trying to think of something to say, you tell them how you came to be on the spaceship.

The tall green aliens look at one another. Finally one says, "It's rather boring, isn't it?" After that they ignore you.

With nothing else to do, you fall asleep by yourself in a corner. The next morning you are awakened by the tall aliens.

"Come and take away this imposter," they are crying at the door. "Its red dots have worn off. They weren't real. And to think we let it associate with us!"

Seventeen rope creatures come in and drag you off to a tiny room by yourself.

One of them says, "Very clever, trying to infiltrate a group returning home. But you'll work a full term of thirty-seven years in the moon mines just as they had to."

THE END

68

Holding your breath, you throw the jewel into the woods, half expecting it to explode. But nothing happens, nothing at all.

Now you wish you'd kept it to show your friends. How else will they believe your strange adventure? Besides, someone would probably pay a fortune for a jewel from another planet. Maybe you could retire before you even had to find a job.

You hunt around for a while, but all you can find is a dull blue stone about the same size as the jewel.

Disappointed, but afraid to go back to the spaceship, you return to school. Will anyone believe your story? If they don't, you could be in trouble for leaving school.

You slip into your next class, ready to explain why you're late. No one looks up. Relieved at first, you sit down at your assigned desk.

But you can't wait to share your adventure. You start telling the entire unbelievable story. Incredibly, nobody pays the slightest bit of attention to you.

It takes awhile before the awful truth hits you. When you threw away the jewel, you became invisible. No one can see or hear you! You wonder how long this awkward condition will last.

THE END

from page 100

"But if this little asteroid crashes into a comet— I mean, we're on this asteroid!" you say to Zax.

"Yes, isn't it exciting!" he says.

Nothing you say will stop Zax from going through with his plan. His machines keep digging up rock and pushing it onto the conveyer belt. Though you try to stop the machines, you can't figure out how. Zax ignores you. He doesn't even seem to care that you're still here. Humming a strange, alien tune, he rushes from machine to machine, making sure everything is running smoothly.

When all is ready, he pushes a lever. Load after load of rocks is flung out into space. Each time the asteroid moves with a terrible jolt.

But Zax has not forgotten you after all. As you helplessly watch the comet come closer and closer, he yells, "See, my plan is wor—"

It's the last thing you hear. You and Zax never find out if the rest of his plan works.

THE END

You choose x-ray vision.

"Here is Robert, your teacher," the alien says. You look down at a boy about three years old. This is your teacher?

But Robert seems to know his subject. First, he teaches you to relax each individual atom in your body. Then he has you stare at a wall, concentrating on each molecule.

Weeks later you can look through the wall at a machine on the other side. You did it! Turning to Robert to tell him the good news, you gasp when you see gears and wheels and wires inside of him. Little Robert is a robot.

Turn to page 81.

from page 22

WE HAVE NO WISH TO HARM EARTHLINGS. OUR INTENTION WAS TO PROGRAM THEM INTO A STATE IN WHICH MISERY WOULD BE AN IMPOSSIBLE CONDITION. BUT AS AN EARTHLING REPRESENTATIVE, IT IS ONLY FAIR THAT YOU DECIDE. BORIUS, TAKE THE EARTHLING TO THE PLANETARY PROGRAMMING CONSOLE.

With one of its branches, Borius hooks you by the collar and steps back into the picture, taking you along. You don't feel any different, but when you glance back at the room you just left, it looks huge. Then Borius sets you down before a small panel in another room and things seem normal size again.

Borius waves a branch at two keys, one red and one blue.

"The blue key leaves things as they are, except for your space program. The red one programs a complete planetary change," Borius explains.

Just to make sure, you ask, "You mean, if I press the red button, everyone on Earth will be happy?"

"Our leader didn't say that," Borius says. "Only that no one could be unhappy."

You wonder if there's a catch there somewhere. Your hand trembles as you slowly aim your finger at a key.

If you press the red key, turn to page 32.

If you press the blue key, turn to page 94.

from page 112

You watch from behind a tree as Strallie returns to the ship and opens the door. After looking carefully inside, she beckons to you, but you don't dare go on board.

You want to call out good-by to her, but you're afraid another alien might hear you. Suddenly something gray is visible behind Strallie. You hear the gray thing clank as though it is metallic. It says something in a strange tongue. But the tone sounds friendly, not angry. As the door closes, Strallie gives a slight wave in your direction.

Soon the craft takes off with a loud roar. A blast of wind forces you to cling to the tree.

Was Strallie really a prisoner? You will always wonder.

THE END

from page 106

You must escape somehow—but how?

The rope creature disappears back into the hole in the wall.

You pace back and forth, your hands in the pockets of your jeans, trying to think of a plan. In one pocket you discover what's left of the red magic marker you were using in the computer room. But what good is that? Suddenly you think of something that might make the aliens voluntarily leave you behind. You're not sure it will work, but the red marker may do the trick.

Then you get another idea. Remembering the hole in the wall, you look through it and see a computer in a tiny room. If you could only get to that computer, maybe you could do something helpful with it. There must be a way to get out of this room. After all, they brought you in here somehow.

If you try your plan with the red marker, turn to page 113.

If you try to get to the computer, turn to page 85.

from page 29

You refuse to answer. The ship is searched and Strallie is discovered. At first angry, the captain later realizes he can make money selling Strallie to an Australian zoo.

You and Strallie are put to work washing pots and pans in the galley. But after worktime is over, you are allowed to swim in the pool and play shuffleboard.

Neither of you can enjoy the journey. Strallie is worried about the zoo. You are worried because you got Strallie into this mess. Besides, the captain told you that your parents are flying over and will meet the ship when it docks.

The evening before the ship is to reach Australia, Strallie tells you she has decided to jump overboard and swim for her freedom as soon as the ship nears the dock.

She asks you to jump overboard with her. You can swim, but you don't know if her plan would work. The captain and his crew always seem to be watching both of you. Maybe you can help Strallie get away if you stay on board.

If you jump ship with Strallie, turn to page 12.

If you stay on board, turn to page 47.

76

To escape is exactly what you want to do, so you quickly jab the ESCAPE key.

The screen prints: THE COMMANDER OF THIS CRAFT IS ORDERED TO LET YOU ESCAPE.

One of the aliens immediately goes to the computer and types something. The screen reads: IT SHALL BE DONE AS ORDERED. Then with a wicked smile, the alien punches the CONTROL key and motions you away from the computer.

With a loud roar, the spaceship takes off and you are all thrown to the floor. After a long time, your head stops spinning and your stomach catches up to the rest of you. "You have to let me escape!" you yell. No one pays any attention to you.

Days go by during which you spend a lot of time playing the game on your wrist watch. You get your score up to astronomical heights. The aliens feed you but otherwise leave you alone.

Finally the ship lands. One of the aliens hands you a box and types a message on the computer screen.

The screen reads: WE WERE ORDERED TO LET YOU ESCAPE, BUT NOT NECESSARILY ON EARTH. YOU MAY NEED THIS TRANSLATOR BOX. PERHAPS WE SHALL RETURN TO FIND OUT HOW YOU ENJOYED YOUR ESCAPE.

Turn to page 53.

"O.K., I'll be your assistant," you say grudgingly to Julia.

After your ship is in space, Julia translates everything she learns from the aliens so you can understand it, too. You learn about astronomy, how to measure vast distances, and much more about the chemistry, physics, and mathematics of outer space.

Mrs. Hardline is kept busy teaching English to the aliens. Norman is assigned to catch anything that gets loose from where it's supposed to be stowed away. Now and then you see him floating around in a space-suit chasing a spoon or a towel.

You never see the alien with the booming voice, though you *hear* it now and then. Finally Julia explains that the voice belongs to their leader, who is too small to be seen. It comes from a different galaxy.

One day the leader sends for you. You wonder what you have done wrong.

"Earthling, we are impressed with how quickly you are learning," the voice says. "Someday your people will travel throughout space just as we do. When that times comes, you will be a valued scientist and diplomat."

From that time on, you are treated as an equal by all the aliens.

THE END

78

Standing perfectly still and looking down, you remind yourself of what to do when facing a strange, angry dog: Don't look it in the eye, because that's a challenge. Just move away slowly.

Cautiously you risk a glance at the lizard. Oh, no! The lizard has been joined by others like it. Noises from behind tell you that you are now probably surrounded by the slimy beasts.

They stand perfectly still, watching you. When you can't stand to remain at attention for another moment, you remember the *Zapping Zombies* game on your wrist watch. It might help to while away the time.

Raising your arms slowly, you press one button twice to get in the game mode, and then the other button to start playing.

Bippety-bip-BEEP-BEEP goes the watch, and you hear the thundering SLAP SLAP SLAP as the lizards jump off in all directions.

"Leaping lizards!" you say in surprise.

By the time the spaceship returns, only the youngest lizards have enough courage to approach you. You play with them until the older ones roar at them. You find the lizards fascinating and would like to learn more about them. The aliens on the ship say you can stay longer if you like.

If you stay on the planet, turn to page 10.

If you get back on the ship, turn to page 56.

from page 16

There is absolutely no resistance—the creature seems to be made of oil. You go sailing through it out the door, landing on the ground with a brain-shaking thud.

Something so heavy lands on top of you that you think the aliens have thrown a weapon in order to kill you. Then you hear Mrs. Hardline say, "I hope I haven't hurt you. When I saw you run, I followed right behind to help you push that alien out of the way."

The spaceship makes a gentle purring sound that turns into a roar. The door again starts to close. You and Mrs. Hardline yell at Julia and Norman to jump.

Julia comes to the door, shouting, "We don't want him along!" and pushes Norman out. Then you see her close the door. The three you run for safety as the ship takes off.

Mrs. Hardline says sadly, "Well, Julia always said she wanted a career in space."

You figure you might also want a career in space someday. But right now it feels great to have your feet planted firmly on the ground.

THE END

Instead of telling Robert about your new power, you think carefully, then say, "What good would it be looking through walls anyway? It can't change anything. I mean, a person couldn't change the controls that steer this ship just by concentrating."

As his gears turn, Robert says, "It is possible, but not permitted. The controls are in the next room, but you can't even see through walls yet."

Soon you are able to use your new powers to turn the ship's controls in the opposite direction. The ship turns. By the time the bewildered aliens are able to figure out why, you are nearly back home.

The gray-haired alien says, "Earthlings are not as simple as we supposed. We will seek another planet to take over."

They let you out near your home, and grant your request to take Robert with you. You figure a little brother who's that smart will be fun.

If you have Robert do your school homework for you, turn to page 60.

If you have Robert teach you after school, turn to page 55.

82

from page 87

"Well, well, well!" says the creature. "So you're still here. You aren't hypnotized. That means you didn't relax as you were told. I'm afraid you will have to stay after all."

"But I don't want to! I'll yell my head off!" you threaten.

The red and yellow disks tremble angrily. "Go right ahead and yell. But if you shout your head off, your head WILL come off. And I don't mind putting you in two separate cages."

"Oh!" you whisper.

"That's better," says the creature, showing you to a cage next to the bear cub. "I think you're going to be good company for me. After we take off, if you're quiet, I'll put you in charge of the cage room and you can play with the other samples."

THE END

84

You want to help Strallie do something useful. But you have no idea what she could do.

You have been teaching Strallie to read. One day you bring her a newspaper. She notices the want ads. "People here have jobs, don't they?" she says. "Your parents have jobs. I'll get one, too."

You help Strallie read the want ads, but you tell her you don't think anyone will hire her. You try to explain that many people on Earth don't feel comfortable around creatures who look different.

"But I'm a nice creature, aren't I?" Strallie asks. "I don't know why anyone wouldn't like me. *I* like me."

She insists on looking for a job. You tell her that without experience her best chance would be at a fast-food restaurant. At Chuck's Chickenburgers, she wouldn't be as conspicuous because all the employees wear clown costumes. Strallie thinks it is a wonderful idea.

The next day you take Strallie to Chuck's.

Chuck takes one look at Strallie and says, "No, I'm sorry. I'm not going to hire you to serve chickenburgers here." Strallie looks very disappointed. You both turn to leave.

Turn to page 63.

from page 74

Wondering how to get to the computer in the next room, you try sticking your finger in the hole in the wall. Amazingly, your whole hand goes through, followed by your arm, and then the rest of you. Now if you can only find some way to make the computer help you.

You press keys on the computer until it turns on. Words fill the screen, but the only one you recognize is PENTAGON. You put your finger on the word. Immediately, the screen clears. Hoping that means the computer is ready for you to send a message to the Pentagon, you type your location and explain about the aliens who want to take over Earth.

Unfortunately, there is no response on the screen. Now what can you do? The only door in this room is locked. Miserably, you sit on the floor to think of another plan. Try as hard as you might, no good ideas come to mind. After a while, the complete silence makes you feel sleepy.

Turn to page 105.

S-Mog opens a cabinet. From a bottom shelf, he hands you a fat, gray gun just like the ones you saw in the film.

"This is as strong a Matter Transmitter Control as we can entrust to a captured Earthling," says S-Mog. "Even I am not permitted to use the one on the top shelf. This is reserved for the Upper Leadership Echelon."

You get a glimpse of a gleaming red gun on the top shelf before S-Mog closes the cabinet.

You don't find aiming the control gun difficult, but distance and timing are tricky. After you learn to move pebbles from a table to a bench, S-Mog leaves you alone in the room. You try to get in the cupboard to get that gun, but can't find a way to open it. As days go by, you are able to move larger and larger objects from room to room.

Then one day you aim the gun at the cupboard. Using all you've learned, you bring out the powerful gun. You promised not to escape from the ship, but you didn't promise not to move the ship.

Sweeping around in a full circle to take in every part of the ship, you aim the Matter Transmitter directly toward Earth. It works!

In less than a moment, you land the ship near your school and escape from the ship. The aliens take off quickly, impressed by our ingenuity.

THE END

Although those shiny red and yellow disks are nearly blinding you, you quickly say, "I'm not here to volunteer. Actually…"

"I'm crushed!" the creature says. All the disks fall in a small heap on the floor. In a moment, they get up and flutter again. "But I can't pass up such a marvelous Earth-sample for my collection. I tell you what," it adds in a kindly tone, "I'll let you look around and get adjusted to your new life before I put you in a cage. Otherwise your wailing would disturb the rest of the collection and it's so hard to get them settled down again. We must have quiet here. But don't worry— you'll grow to love being part of my collection."

"But you don't want me for your collection!" you say, thinking frantically. "I'm very noisy."

"Well, you can't leave now," the creature says. "You would report us, and we would have to leave before I could get more samples. So just look around quietly."

At the top of your lungs you scream, "I won't be quiet! I won't be quiet! I won't be quiet!" From the cages there is a great screeching and bellowing.

"Oh, very well," says the creature crossly. "I suppose I can hypnotize you so you won't remember being here. Then you will be free to go. Just look at me and relax."

If you let yourself be hypnotized, turn to page 19.

If you only pretend to be hypnotized, turn to page 82.

88

The key you desperately hit is the CONTROL key.

Immediately the aliens freeze helplessly. The computer screen reads: YOU ARE IN CONTROL. PRESS ANOTHER KEY TO EXECUTE COMMAND.

The guards are only one step away from you, motionless, staring murderously at you. You know you'd better not make a wrong move. But what would a helpful key be in this situation?

Remembering that some computers have a HELP key, you search quickly and breathe a sigh of relief as you find one. You press the HELP key.

The screen writes: NOTE OPERATIONAL KEYS AS INDICATED.

What kind of help is that? Then you see that four keys are now lit up: RESET, DELETE, PAUSE, and ESCAPE.

Which key should you press?

If you hit RESET, turn to page 18.

If you hit DELETE, turn to page 6.

If you hit PAUSE, turn to page 24.

If you hit ESCAPE, turn to page 76.

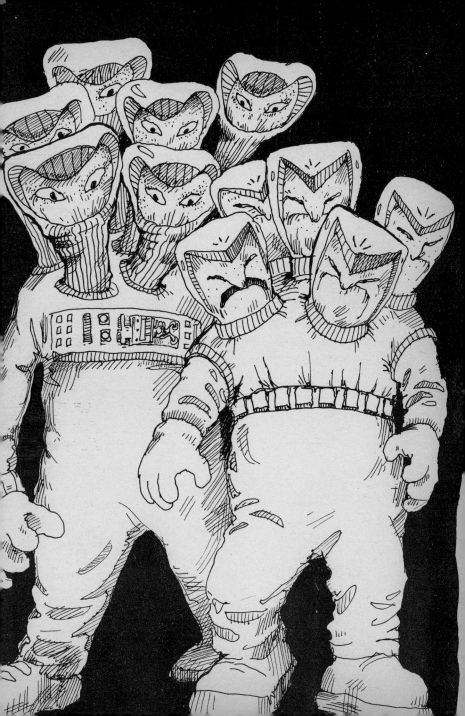

90

"Will I really be the first to explore the planet?" you ask Borius. "That's quite an honor."

"Well, actually," Borius admits, "our Command Council told me you were selected because no one knows whether or not the planet is dangerous."

"I don't think I want to go," you say.

"The decision has already been made," Borius says. "We will return soon to get a report from you, if you are still able to give one."

Borius gives you a small, metal box and explains, "This is a computerized translator box in case there are inhabitants that are not evolved enough to communicate with you." The spacecraft lands on the newly discovered planet.

Turn to page 53.

Mrs. Hardline says she will be glad to help.

You figure she is really going to give it to Norman. But instead you hear her say to him kindly, "Norman, I know you are scared and homesick. We all are." They have a long talk.

After that Norman does much better. Soon you let him take over your job as well, as Julia promised you could. But that doesn't last long. He starts goofing off again and complaining. So the two of you work side by side.

Finally you find that you and Norman are competing to see who can work harder.

Your alien captors are so pleased with your performances that they decide to keep you there even after the other workers are sent home.

THE END

The short green aliens ask how you came to be captured. After listening to your tale of woe, they confer in a strange language.

Finally one says, "We are returning home after working in the moon mines for thirty-seven years. In the mines, we learned your language from captured Earthlings. You will suffer the same sad fate unless you come to live on our planet. We will try to help you."

You thank them for their offer.

In the morning you are awakened by a short green alien whispering in your ear, "Your red dots are all gone. Can you replace them before the guards see you?" Quickly you take out the red marker and add more dots to your face and hands.

Soon the ship lands, and you and the green creatures are let off. Your new friends build you a little red cottage, and plant you a garden of strange but delicious red vegetables.

It's a happy new life, but you dream of the day when you can return home. You picture your entire home town turning out to greet you with bands and fireworks.

THE END

from page 43

Is it safe to go right up to the strange vehicle? You decide you'd better watch it for a while to see what happens.

Standing behind a tree at the edge of the clearing, you keep your eyes glued to the craft. There are windows in it, but you don't see anyone looking out.

And yet you have a spooky feeling that *you* are being watched!

The feeling gets stronger and stronger. Suddenly you whirl around. Behind a nearby bush you see two eyes staring at you.

You run away as fast as you can. Turning around to look over your shoulder, you crash into a tree and fall down.

Then you hear something jumping towards you through the woods, closer and closer!

Turn to page 20.

from page 72

As you press down on the blue button, you are immediately transported back to school. There you tell Mr. Twill, your social-studies teacher, that some aliens in the woods are going to stop the U.S. space program.

He says sternly, "You think this nonsense tale is going to make me overlook the fact that you didn't do your mapping assignment? I've been teaching much too long for that. What were you doing in the computer room, playing video games again? Just take your seat and be prepared to do extra homework for the next two weeks!"

On your next report card is a note from Mr. Twill: "Has vivid imagination which needs to be properly channeled."

The news headlines go on as before, except that no country seems to be able to get its space program off the ground. You wish that Earth would hurry up and get over the Age of Agression. The aliens did it, so you figure there's hope for your planet, too.

THE END

You decide to let Julia take care of this problem. Without waiting to untie the rest of you, she opens the hatch in the wall and climbs into a tunnel.

You wait impatiently for her to return and set you free. Norman whispers to you, "You got us into this mess. Why don't you get us out of it?"

You hear Mrs. Hardline struggling to get free. Finally she gives up in exhaustion. You whisper to her, "I guess we'll suffer now AND suffer later."

She whispers back, "I was a teacher long before I became a principal. If we do go into space, at least your education will not suffer."

Sighing, you wonder how long Julia has been gone. You can't see your watch, so you start counting off the seconds, "One million, two million, three million...."

Suddenly there is a terrible jolt, a loud roar, and you feel like you're on a roller coaster zooming up instead of down. The effect on your stomach is the same—you feel awful. It looks like Julia did not take care of anything.

As the three of you look at each other in dismay, you realize that the only people from Earth you can talk to for the rest of your life are Norman, Julia, and Mrs. Hardline.

URK!

THE END

from page 61

You figure a lot of people would love to travel into space. But would one of them be willing to make it a one-way trip?

As you climb down the ladder, Strallie says, "You or your substitute must be back here in one hour. If not, I'm afraid it won't be pleasant for you."

On the way back to school, you think desperately. How in the world can you find a substitute in one hour?

In school, classes are changing and the hall is full of students. Norman Stillman, the school nerd, says, "Where were you? I happened to mention to the hall monitor that you left. You're supposed to report to the principal's office." He laughs long and loud.

You say to Norman angrily, "It's none of your business where I've been."

Showing a fist, Norman asks, "You want a knuckle sandwich?"

"There's a spaceship in the woods," you whisper. "But stay away from it."

"I see. You want to hog all the glory," Norman says.

You walk away without replying. After a moment you turn and see Norman running toward the back door of the school.

You yell at him to stop, but he keeps running. "Well, I did warn him not to!" you say to yourself.

THE END

You yell at Norman until you develop laryngitis, but it doesn't do the slightest bit of good. Now you have to work so hard doing both jobs, you barely have time for sleep. Mrs. Hardline works as hard as she can, but it isn't enough.

And all the while, Norman complains and whines. Finally the aliens lose patience with him and send him home.

You and Mrs. Hardline look at each other. You don't have to say what you are thinking.

"Oh, my aching back!" moans Mrs. Hardline, walking around stooped over.

"My shoulder is stiff," you whine, standing with one shoulder higher than the other. "How can I work this way?"

The next morning, Mrs. Hardline shouts, "I stubbed my toe!" She hops around pathetically on one foot.

"I'm allergic to moon dust!" you groan between coughing spells.

Every hour you each have a different ailment that prevents you from working.

Soon you are on the next spaceship bound for Earth.

THE END

from page 9

"Dear Mom and Dad," you write, "I don't know how to tell you this, so I will just tell you. I am on a spaceship heading for an unknown galaxy. I'm not sure when or if I can return, so please feed my fish." Your parents have always complained about your letters from camp, but you don't have the knack to put everything you'd like into words.

Weeks go by during which you keep busy studying the mathematics of fuel propulsion. One day Borius tells you, "We're stopping at an asteroid station to pick up oxygen to add to our fuel."

After the ship lands, you and Borius get off for a stroll on the tiny, barren planet. You are greeted by a creature so covered with long hair that you can't tell what shape the creature itself is.

"How are you coming with your planet-moving project, Zax?" Borius asks.

"I'm just about ready," Zax replies. "Is this the apprentice I asked you for?"

Borius takes you aside and says, "I'm not sure if Zax is crazy or brilliant. That's why we left him here alone to carry on his strange project. You can stay and learn from him, or continue with us and be the first to explore a newly discovered planet."

If you stay with Zax, turn to page 23.

If you continue with Borius, turn to page 90.

from page 23

"Yes, indeed," Zax says. "And when the comet crashes into the moon, that force will move the moon close enough to pull a planet into a new course near my home planet. It will make it more convenient for me to study that planet, and to be able to go home frequently."

You wonder if it's a planet you've heard of. "What planet is going to be moved?" you ask.

"The one its inhabitants refer to as Earth," he says. "I hear it's full of interesting machines."

Your head is spinning. You're not sure, but you suspect his plan will be disastrous for the inhabitants of Earth. And when the asteroid you're on crashes into the comet, you don't think it's going to be too healthy for you two either.

If you point out the danger to Earth, turn to page 114.

If you point out the danger to you and Zax, turn to page 69.

"O.K., I promise not to try to escape from the ship," you say, not mentioning that you would like to destroy it.

The rope alien coils itself around you as you gasp for breath. You become thin enough to fit through the hole in the wall. The rope alien takes you to another room where you return to your normal size. After a few moments of dizziness, you look around.

The Learning Lab is filled with silent beings, sitting or standing perfectly still, with their eyes closed or fixed in a glazed stare. You think a few are Earthlings.

Facing you is an alien with floor-length gray hair and beard. Through its hair you see a curly blue nose, with one pale yellow eye just above it.

"I would introduce you," says the gray alien, who seems to be in charge, "but they are working so hard, it would be a shame to interrupt them. Total concentration is the path to the powers you will learn here. I'm afraid we only have two openings right now: x-ray vision or transport. Do you have a preference?"

With x-ray vision, perhaps you could learn to see through the machinery on this ship and figure out how to alter it. Transport sounds like busses and trains. You don't like to admit your ignorance to your kidnappers.

If you choose x-ray vision, turn to page 70.

If you choose transport, turn to page 49.

from page 57

Your arm feels heavy as you lift your hand. As soon as you touch the surprisingly warm jewel, you feel your strength returning. Your brain is filled with a single purpose: To bring others here to talk to the Voice.

Still floating, you feel yourself propelled through the fog until you land with a slight jolt on something firm. The fog disappears. You see that you are just below a ladder attached to a strange, three-legged craft. Now you know where you are—the clearing in the woods that you sometimes use as a short cut to school. Quickly you set out to bring other people here. But the farther you get from the craft in the woods, the more clearly you can think.

"Am I mixed up in something dangerous?" you ask yourself, now that the strangeness of the situation is becoming clear to you. "Is it right to involve other people in it?"

You stop for a moment to think things through. Immediately hot sparks fly from the jewel in your hand. Terrified, you almost drop it. That starts you thinking again. Maybe it would be a good idea to let go of the jewel. Or could harm come to you if you get rid of it? After all, you accepted it as part of an agreement.

If you get rid of the jewel, turn to page 68.

If you keep the jewel, turn to page 14.

from page 11

The wall slides open, revealing a row of computers. You can only read one of the labels above them: PLANET EARTH COMMUNICATIONS.

Hoping against hope, you turn the computer on and enter the network number of the school's computers.

Frantically you type as fast as you can: HELP! MRS. HARDLINE I MEAN HARDING AND NORMAN AND I ARE BEING HELD CAPTIVE IN A SPACESHIP. CONTACT THE SPACE PROGRAM AND ASK IF THEY CAN SEND A SHIP TO RESCUE US. You know it's a slim hope that they can send something up so quickly.

You look up to find Julia at your side. Furiously she pounds some keys on the same computer. "O.K., I'll send you back," she says angrily. "But if you try to give me away, no one will believe you."

The next moment you are in front of a computer at school with your message on the screen. You see it's on the other screens, too. A boy yells at you, "Keep your dumb story off our screens!" Norman is at the computer behind you, looking pale. Julia is standing by the door, glaring at you. Mrs. Hardline walks by the room, looking as confused as you feel.

You don't understand how Julia did it, but you are glad to be back!

THE END

from page 85

Suddenly a crashing sound jolts you awake. The door to the room bursts open and several men in business suits enter. One of them holds out an I.D. card with the letters F.B.I. on it.

Before you can speak, the man with the card says, "Kids again! Nice little playhouse you've got here. But breaking into the Pentagon's network is no joke! We're confiscating your computer." He and the other agents lead you out.

"But this is a spaceship. That rope in the corner is an alien," you say, pointing at the only thing left in the little spaceship.

"Sure, kid," one of the men says. The F.B.I. agents march you back to school. As you walk back through the woods, you hear a dull roar behind you. You and the men turn to see the ship take off and zoom away.

The men look at you with new respect. Now they are ready to listen to what you have to say. You are just glad to be safe on Earth.

THE END

106

from page 109

For a while there is silence. This gives you a brief chance to explore the room. Searching desperately, all you can find is a small hole in one wall. Before you can look through it, a rope slips through the opening, then stands upright in front of you.

"Hello!" says a high, piping voice.

"A rope that speaks English!" you say.

"I've spent a lot of time on your planet," the rope creature says. "Earthlings never suspect me, so I'm able to learn a great deal."

"But why do you come here and watch us?" you ask. Now you notice one little eye at the top of the rope.

The rope says, "I guess there's no harm in telling you. If you try to escape, I will tie you up. We are going home now to report that Earth is ready for takeover. Some Earthlings will work in our space mines. All others will be put to work providing the raw materials we need until your resources are exhausted. We will take off shortly and I have some loose ends to tie up, so I'll leave you for a while. Remember that any attempt to escape is useless—and dangerous."

You must foil their plans to take over the Earth! But what should you do?

If you try to find some way to escape, to warn the authorities, turn to page 74.

If you stay to try to prevent the ship from leaving, turn to page 15.

The four of you are silent.

"ARE YOU TYPICAL?" the voice asks, and again the whole room seems to tremble.

You and Norman and Julia and Mrs. Hardline all look at each other. Then Mrs. Hardline says to the rest of you, "I'll handle this. First of all, we won't answer any questions until we know to whom we are talking."

"SILENCE!" thunders the voice. The floor shakes so hard that the four of you have to grab each other to keep from falling.

"I WANT AN ANSWER FROM THE ONE WHO CAME HERE FIRST. THE ONE WHO REFUSED TO OBEY INSTRUCTIONS NOT TO GET INVOLVED," says the voice.

You remember the message that appeared on your computer screen:

EXPERIMENT—INTRUDER—INTERCEPTED
DO NOT CONTINUE

Mrs. Hardline and Julia and Norman glare at you.

"ARE YOU TYPICAL EARTHLINGS?" the voice asks again.

You look at the others—the school nerd, the school brain, the principal. You think about yourself, too. Are you typical? You have no idea, but you're afraid to say you don't know.

If you say you are typical Earthlings, turn to page 42.

If you say you are not typical, turn to page 65.

108

You dive behind a chair and watch from there. Then it hits you. You're looking at a film—a very realistic three-dimensional film. There isn't really anyone in the corner.

Marching boldly up to the 3-D picture, you see a box in front of it with buttons labeled Francais, Espanol, Deutsch, English, and the names of many other languages. You press the English button and hear the man say, "We must set up a permanent space colony before THEY do. Even if their government does not act quickly, some of their real-estate agents will blast off and start selling lunar tracts to alien creatures!"

Ordinarily, you would find this amusing. But something serious is happening. Someone is able to photograph and listen in on people in the space programs of more than one government, including the United States. And you may be the only one who's aware of it. It's up to you to do something. But what?

If you want to leave the ship to contact someone in the U.S. space program, turn to page 38.

If you want to stay here to learn more about who is doing the spying, turn to page 30.

109

from page 57

Concentrating with great difficulty, you murmur, "I can't bring other people here until I can see you and see where I am."

After a brief silence, the fog gradually lifts. You are all alone in a tiny room with metal walls and a low ceiling.

Finally the Voice, which seems to come from all directions at once, says: YOU DO NOT OBEY ORDERS AND ARE THEREFORE UNSUITABLE FOR RECRUITING. FOR THE PAST THIRTY YEARS, OUR PLANETARIANS HAVE BEEN OBSERVING EARTH. WE ARE NOT READY TO ANNOUNCE OUR PRESENCE YET. YOU MUST ACCOMPANY US WHEN WE LEAVE. YOU WILL NOT BE MISTREATED IF YOU COOPERATE.

Your mind is feeling sharper. But the more clearly you can think, the more frightened you become.

The rumbling Voice says: MAKE YOURSELF COMFORTABLE. WE WILL BE TAKING OFF SOON. I HAVE NO MORE TIME TO TALK TO YOU BUT I WILL SEND SOMEONE TO KEEP YOU COMPANY.

Turn to page 106.

110

Immediately words appear on the screen in English: WE WILL BE TAKING OFF SOON.

Is the computer talking to you? You glance at the aliens by the door, but they still have their backs to you. One says something in the alien language. As it talks, more words appear on the screen: WHAT ARE THE PLANS FOR THAT ALIEN?

Could the computer be translating what they say? You wonder what alien they are talking about.

The other alien speaks and the screen prints: I HEAR IT HESITATES AND THINKS BEFORE ACTING, SO IT IS OF NO USE TO US. IT IS ONLY AN EARTHLING. IT WILL PROBABLY BE PAIN-LESSLY DISINTEGRATED.

As you realize what alien they are discussing—*you* —your teeth begin to chatter from fright.

As the other alien replies, the screen writes: IT NEVER HURTS TO BE KIND, AND DISINTEGRA-TION IS NOT MESSY. BUT WHAT IS THAT CLICKING SOUND?

Your teeth won't stop chattering. Turning in your direction, the aliens yell, and the screen prints: GET IT AWAY FROM THAT COMPUTER!

The aliens rush at you. Desperately you push another key.

Turn to page 88.

"My name is Borius," the creature says. "We'll be taking off soon. Since you're three-dimensional, you'd better get strapped in."

"Oh, I have to get home for dinner," you say.

"You may go home if you wish. But have you ever been to the moon? It's only a short hop away," Borius says.

The moon? *That* would be a story for the school paper! In fact, you could get into every newspaper in the country.

If you stay on board, turn to page 9.

If you insist on leaving the ship, turn to page 22.

112

"Strallie, I wish I could tell you that you'd be treated well here, but I can't guarantee it," you say. "You would cause a terrific amount of excitement. You'd be mobbed by reporters and crowds of people wanting a look at you. I don't know what the government's attitude would be—whether they'd protect you or not. They'd certainly want to talk to you."

"I don't think I'd like all that excitement," Strallie says. "I've been living a quiet life for the past several hundred years. Actually, I'm so used to living in the spaceship that I guess I'll just go back. It's really not an unpleasant life."

"Are you sure that's what you want?" you ask.

"I think so," says Strallie. "Why don't you come and take a look inside? The others are all busy in the front of the ship preparing for takeoff. That's how I was able to escape."

This is the chance of a lifetime. You'd be famous as the first person on Earth to set foot inside a spaceship from another planet!

But what if the other aliens see you, and take you captive as they did Strallie?

If you go inside the spaceship, turn to page 27.

If you reluctantly say no, turn to page 73.

With the red marker, you put red dots all over your face and hands. You plan to tell the aliens that you are ill with something contagious, so they won't take you along. Banging on the walls to get their attention, you wait impatiently for the rope alien to return.

Instead, the ship roars and takes off!

You're too late. Should you try your plan anyway? You could tell the aliens it isn't safe to take over Earth because a red-dotted plague is going around. Or should you try to think of something else?

If you tell the aliens about the plague, turn to page 44.

If you try to think of something else, turn to page 52.

"But won't all the people on Earth be destroyed?" you ask Zax.

He looks thoughtful for a moment. "Well, yes, I suppose they will. But think of all I will learn from the experiment," he points out. "Now you let me know when the bucket fills up. We're ready to start. I'll be at the controls."

"I won't help you!" you say. "I'll stop you somehow!"

With a furious roar, Zax lunges for you. You start climbing up the machine to get away from him, but he follows. Leaping from rock to rock on the conveyer belt, you struggle to keep your balance. You jump into the bucket and run along the long, slippery metal arm.

Zax is slower than you. When you get to the machinery at the other end of the arm, you look back and see Zax climbing out of the bucket onto the arm. As you jump to the ground, your foot hits a lever and pushes it down. You have to duck quickly as the long arm starts swinging around, faster and faster.

Suddenly a huge load of rocks goes spinning silently out into space, along with the hairy inventor. The asteroid moves in the opposite direction with a terrific jolt. Then everything is still. You have saved Earth!

In a few days, a spaceship stops by for oxygen. The crew agrees to take you home.

THE END

116

from page 50

You are having trouble breathing.

Julia looks startled when she sees you. Rushing to the tunnel entrance, she says, "Get back! You can't breathe in here." She follows you back to the room where you left Mrs. Hardline and Norman. Speaking to you quietly so no one else can hear, she says, "This area has Earth atmosphere. But I can get along in both environments. I'm what you call an alien. My mother came here on an earlier mission and married an Earthling."

"You have no right to keep me here," you say.

Julia replies, "I was trying to obtain your release. But now that you know about me, you must come with us. We can't risk having you give me away. I'll be going back to Earth. We obtain some of the raw materials we need here, so my presence is useful."

"What if I promise not to tell anyone?" you plead.

"We couldn't take the chance," Julia says. "Look, if you don't cause any trouble, you can be my assistant and learn a great deal about outer space."

You are angry with Julia. But should you make the best of a bad situation and become her assistant?

If you become Julia's assistant, turn to page 77.

If you refuse, turn to page 11.